MT. PLEASANT LIBRARY
PLEASANTVILLE, NY
W9-BQS-785

# Dear Mr. President

For Emile, Oliver, and Lilka, who all know what
it's like to share a room! – SS

For Willian, Nathan, Alexis, and Maxime – AV

# Dear Mr. President

Sophie Siers
Anne Villeneuve

Owlkids Books

Dear Mr. President,

I'm writing you a letter from my bedroom. Sadly, the room does not belong only to me. I have to share it with my big brother, who exactly fits your description of an undesirable person.

I watched you on the TV news tonight, and you said you were building a wall. It made me think that perhaps I need one too.

Yours faithfully,

Sam

Dear Mr. President,

The problem is that my brother has a phone, and he plays on it at night even though he isn't allowed. It keeps me awake. I suggested to Mom and Dad that they let me build a wall across the room.

They said no.

Very sincerely,

Sam

Dear Mr. President,

At dinner tonight we had a discussion about the wall proposals, both yours and mine. I don't know about you, but I'm getting a lot of negative feedback.

My brother said that they're both dumb ideas.

Mom said that if you were like other men she knew, you would talk about a wall a lot but never build one.

Dad didn't say anything.

Respectfully,

Sam

Dear Mr. President,

Everybody was talking about your wall at school today. There didn't seem to be many kids who thought it was a good idea.

They obviously don't know what it's like to share a room.

Our teacher, Mr. Green, has given us a project on "Great Walls of the World." He said that some of them didn't quite work to plan. I told him that mine definitely would!

Yours truly,

Sam

Dear Mr. President,

Dad took my brother and me fishing today.

He wanted to talk about the wall.

He said we needed to talk things over and see if we could "negotiate" a way to make things work in our room.

I told him that actions speak louder than words.

I thought that's the sort of thing you'd say in my situation.

Best regards,

Dear Mr. President,

I've discovered I'm great at building walls! I've built two in the garden and one that went right across the pond, which made a dam as well. I made them out of sand and stones, and Dad said my best one looked like The Great Wall of China!

He told me that the wall in China was the biggest wall ever made and was built to hold back marauding invaders.

It's exactly what I need.

Your friend,

Dear Mr. President,

My brother is behaving like a marauding invader.
This morning he took my Star Wars Destroyer.
That means war.

I told my mom that this could have been
averted if she had let me build a wall, but she
just LAUGHED!

I bet no one is laughing at <u>your</u> wall idea.

Good night, from

# SAM

Dear Mr. President,

I borrowed some books from the library to help me with my wall project. The Great Wall of China is humongous! Mom's favorite is a really old one in Zimbabwe.

Hadrian's Wall, which went right across England, was 84 miles long! My room is only 13 feet wide—I don't understand why building my wall is such a big deal.

Yours frustratedly,

SAM -

Dear Mr. President,

At school today my best friend, Robert Burns, told me you could see The Great Wall of China from space, but Bella said that wasn't true.

I think I'll be an astronaut when I grow up, then I can see for myself.

Did you want to be a wall builder when you were a kid?

All the best,

SAM

Dear Mr. President,

I stayed with my grandma this weekend. It's great staying there because I get my own room, and Gran lets me do pretty much whatever I want.

The downside was that there were some strange noises in the night. I lay awake counting the walls between my room and Gran's.

. . . . . . . . 4 . . . . . . . . . . . 5 . . . . . . . . . . 6

There are six. I counted them a lot of times.

Bye for now,

Sam

Dear Mr. President,

There has obviously been some "dialogue" while I was away. My brother is using words like "harmony" and "spirit of sharing" and suggesting that a wall is not needed.

I, however, remain unconvinced.

Later,

-SAM

Dear Mr. President,

I'm still the only one in the house who thinks that the wall is a good idea.

I'm committed to getting it done even if my big brother did "ask" to borrow my pocket knife (he's <u>never</u> asked before), and last night he even went under the covers to use his phone!

Best,

Sam

Dear Mr. President,

I'm having second thoughts about the wall.

Yesterday, my brother put my clean laundry on my bed (he usually dumps it on the floor). I said thank you and returned the cap I borrowed from him a few weeks ago. Things are much better.

At dinner Dad said he was proud of us and told a very long story about a wall in Berlin that got knocked down. He said that communication and negotiation are always preferable to separation.

I kind of see what he means.

See ya,

sam

Dear Mr. President,

I'm really sorry, but I'm dropping the whole wall idea.
To cut a long story short, a big brother in your room is
pretty cool when you've just had the worst nightmare
ever. I'm glad I didn't get around to building it.

I feel a bit silly changing my mind, but my brother says it's cool, and Mom said she admires a man who admits when he's wrong.

Dad didn't say anything.

Anyway, good luck with your wall.

Perhaps a small one would do?

Best wishes,

Text © 2019 Sophie Siers
Illustrations © 2019 Anne Villeneuve

Originally published by Millwood Press Ltd, New Zealand
North American edition published 2019 by Owlkids Books Inc.

All rights reserved. No part of this publication may be reproduced, stored in a retrieval system,
or transmitted in any form or by any means, without the prior written permission of Owlkids
Books Inc., or in the case of photocopying or other reprographic copying, a license from the
Canadian Copyright Licensing Agency (Access Copyright). For an Access Copyright license,
visit www.accesscopyright.ca or call toll-free to 1-800-893-5777.

Owlkids Books acknowledges the financial support of the Canada Council for the Arts,
the Ontario Arts Council, the Government of Canada through the Canada Book Fund (CBF)
and the Government of Ontario through the Ontario Creates Book Initiative
for our publishing activities.

Published in Canada by Owlkids Books Inc., 1 Eglinton Avenue East, Toronto, ON M4P 3A1
Published in the US by Owlkids Books Inc., 1700 Fourth Street, Berkeley, CA 94710

Library of Congress Control Number: 2018965187

Library and Archives Canada Cataloguing in Publication

Siers, Sophie, 1969- [Dear Donald Trump]
Dear Mr. President / Sophie Siers ; [illustrated by] Anne Villeneuve.

ISBN 978-1-77147-391-0 (hardcover)
I. Villeneuve, Anne, 1966-, illustrator  II. Title.
III.Title: Dear Donald Trump

PZ7.1.S54Dea 2019          j823'.92          C2018-906590-7

Manufactured in Dongguan, China, in February 2019, by
Toppan Leefung Packaging & Printing (Dongguan) Co. Ltd.
Job #BAYDC65

A          B          C          D          E          F

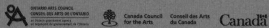

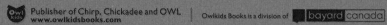